COUNTRY PROFILES

IRAN

BY ALICIA Z. KLEPEIS

BLASTOFF!
DISCOVERY

BELLWETHER MEDIA • MINNEAPOLIS, MN

Blastoff! Discovery launches
a new mission: reading to learn.
Filled with facts and features, each
book offers you an exciting new
world to explore!

This edition first published in 2020 by Bellwether Media, Inc.

No part of this publication may be reproduced in whole or in part
without written permission of the publisher.
For information regarding permission, write to Bellwether Media, Inc.,
Attention: Permissions Department,
6012 Blue Circle Drive, Minnetonka, MN 55343.

Library of Congress Cataloging-in-Publication Data

Names: Klepeis, Alicia, 1971- author.
Title: Iran / Alicia Z. Klepeis.
Other titles: Blastoff! discovery. Country profiles.
Description: Minneapolis, MN : Bellwether Media, Inc., 2020. |
    Series: Blastoff discovery. Country profiles | Includes
    bibliographical references and index. | Audience: Grades 3-8 |
    Audience: Ages 7-13 | Summary: "Engaging images accompany
    information about Iran. The combination of high-interest subject
    matter and narrative text is intended for students in grades 3
    through 8"– Provided by publisher.
Identifiers: LCCN 2019034849 (print) | LCCN 2019034850 (ebook)
    | ISBN 9781644871690 (library binding) | ISBN
    9781618918451 (ebook)
Subjects: LCSH: Iran–Juvenile literature.
Classification: LCC DS254.75 .K58 2020 (print) | LCC DS254.75
    (ebook) | DDC 955–dc23
LC record available at https://lccn.loc.gov/2019034849
LC ebook record available at https://lccn.loc.gov/2019034850

Editor: Rebecca Sabelko   Designer: Brittany McIntosh

Printed in the United States of America, North Mankato, MN.

TABLE OF CONTENTS

PERSEPOLIS

It is a warm summer morning in the ancient city of Persepolis. A group of schoolchildren arrives, ready to explore the ruins. Persepolis was once the capital of the **Persian** Empire. A guide takes them to see the 2,500-year-old carvings on the city's stone walls. Many carvings show people delivering goods to their king. Others show the local plants and animals.

OTHER TOP SITES

BADAB-E SURT

ERAM GARDENS

MOUNT DAMAVAND

SHAH MOSQUE

The students wander among the city's ruins until lunchtime. The tall columns loom overhead. After lunch, the children visit the tomb of the Persian king Artaxerxes II. They enjoy a beautiful view of the city below. Welcome to Iran!

Iran is located in the **Middle East**. It covers 636,372 square miles (1,648,195 square kilometers). Tehran, the country's capital, lies in the north. Iran's second-largest city, Mashhad, is in the northeast.

Iran has many land neighbors. To the north are Armenia, Azerbaijan, and Turkmenistan. Afghanistan and Pakistan border Iran to the east. The nations of Iraq and Turkey make up the western border. Approximately one-third of Iran's borders are coasts. The Caspian Sea washes against Iran's northern coast. The waters of the Gulf of Oman and the Persian Gulf form Iran's southern coast.

TURKMENISTAN

CASPIAN
SEA

TEHRAN

KARAJ

MASHHAD

IRAN

ESFAHAN

AFGHANISTAN

SHIRAZ

PAKISTAN

PERSIAN
GULF

GULF
OF OMAN

Much of Iran is high in **elevation**. The middle of the country is a high **plateau**. This plateau is home to the Kavir and Lut Deserts. The Zagros Mountains run from Iran's northwestern borders to the **Strait** of Hormuz. The Elburz Mountains in the north stretch from the Caspian Sea's southern shores to eastern Iran. The nation's coastal regions are flatter than the rest of the country.

= KAVIR DESERT   = ELBURZ MOUNTAINS
= LUT DESERT   = ZAGROS MOUNTAINS

LUT DESERT

TEHRAN

Average seasonal highs and lows

JANUARY
HIGH: 47 °F (8 °C)
LOW: 33 °F (0.6 °C)

APRIL
HIGH: 72 °F (22 °C)
LOW: 54 °F (12 °C)

JULY
HIGH: 99 °F (37 °C)
LOW: 77 °F (25 °C)

OCTOBER
HIGH: 76 °F (24 °C)
LOW: 57 °F (14 °C)

°F = degrees Fahrenheit
°C = degrees Celsius

EARTH SHATTERING!

Earthquakes occur often in Iran. They are frequently quite violent and cause a lot of damage. A 2018 earthquake in western Iran was even felt across the border into Iraq!

Most of Iran has a dry climate. Temperatures can be very cold or hot, depending on the season and location. The area by the Caspian Sea has a wetter **subtropical** climate.

9

Iran's landscape is filled with wildlife! Wild goats and brown bears make their homes in the remote mountains, while cat snakes search for lizards to eat. Deer graze on plants as foxes hunt for rodents in Iran's semidesert areas. Striped hyenas live in many regions of Iran. They largely feed on **carrion**.

Seagulls and terns dwell along Iran's coasts. Whales and dolphins live in the Persian Gulf while Caspian seals thrive in the Caspian Sea's less salty waters. These bodies of water are also home to a wide variety of fish.

BROWN BEAR

CAT SNAKE

CORSAC FOX

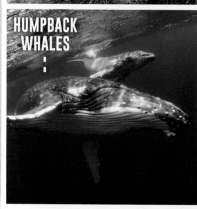

HUMPBACK WHALES

ROE DEER

STRIPED
HYENA

LITTLE AFRICA

Kavir National Park is often called "Little Africa." The nickname is due to the wildlife, such as hyenas and gazelles, found in the park.

STRIPED HYENA

Life Span: up to 12 years
Red List Status: near threatened

striped hyena range =

LEAST CONCERN	NEAR THREATENED	VULNERABLE	ENDANGERED	CRITICALLY ENDANGERED	EXTINCT IN THE WILD	EXTINCT

More than 83 million people live in Iran. Most Iranians belong to the Persian **ethnic** group. Smaller groups of people include Azeris, Kurds, Lurs, Balochs, and **Arabs**. Some of these groups live a **nomadic** lifestyle. However, more and more of Iran's nomads are moving to cities.

Nearly everyone in Iran is Muslim. Most follow the Shi'a branch of Islam rather than the Sunni branch. Fewer than 1 out of 100 Iranians follow a religion other than Islam. They may practice Christianity or Judaism. The official language of Iran is Persian, which is also known as Farsi.

FAMOUS FACE

Name: Shirin Ebadi
Birthday: June 21, 1947
Hometown: Tehran, Iran
Famous for: One of the first women in Iran to serve as a judge and in 2003, won Iran's first Nobel Peace Prize

SPEAK PERSIAN, OR FARSI

Persian, also called Farsi, uses script instead of letters. However, Persian words can be written with the English alphabet so you can read them.

ENGLISH	PERSIAN (FARSI)	HOW TO SAY IT
hello	sâlam	sah-LAAM
goodbye	khodâ hâfez	kho-DAH hah-fez
please	lotfan	loht-FAHN
thank you	mamnoon	maam-NOON
yes	baleh	BAH-leh
no	nakheyr	NEK-hay-er

ESFAHAN

COMMUNITIES

About three-quarters of all Iranians live in **urban** areas. Most middle-class people dwell in apartments typically made of cement, bricks, and stone. Wealthier Iranians may live in fancy homes with big yards and swimming pools. People in Tehran often travel by car, bus, train, or foot.

Rural homes are often made of wood, cement, or brick. Tents are common among nomadic tribes. People in the countryside may travel on foot, by bus, or by car.

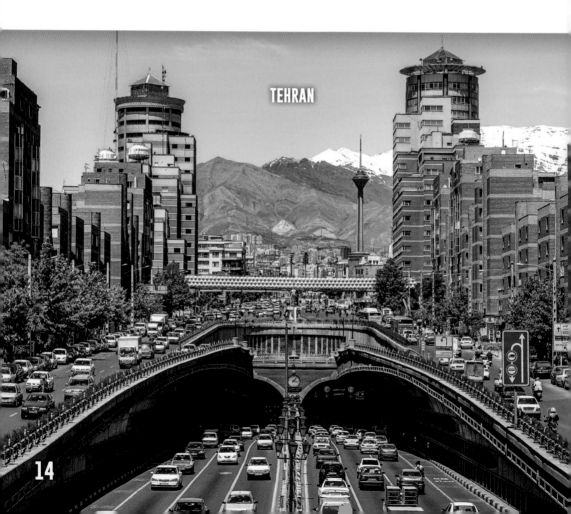

TEHRAN

COLOR AND CARPETS

Most Iranian homes have colorful carpets. Some carpet designs are connected with a specific tribe or town. Other patterns may be passed down in a carpet-making family.

NOMADIC TENT

Family plays an important role in the lives of Iranian people. An average family has two children. Grandparents commonly provide childcare when parents are working.

HAPPY CLOTHES

The Gilaki people live in Iran's northern Gilan province. Women traditionally wear long skirts with colorful stripes, embroidered jackets, and headdresses. Gilaki men wear trousers, wide cotton belts, shirts, vests, and woolly hats.

Iranians are known for being friendly and polite. Most people greet each other by saying *sâlam,* meaning "peace." Handshakes are common. However, a man will not shake a woman's hand unless she offers it to him. People of the same gender in Iran will say hello by kissing each other on the cheek.

People in Iran usually wear **conservative** clothing when in public. Women must be completely covered, except for their hands and face. Iranian women often wear a long outer garment called a *chador*. Most also wear makeup and jewelry. Younger people commonly wear jeans and T-shirts.

CHADORS

Students in Iran start six years of primary school at age 6. Most students then go on to attend secondary school. During the last three years of secondary school, students can study literature, science, and the arts to prepare for university. They can also choose a **vocational** path of study.

Nearly half of all Iranians have **service jobs**. Some people work in banks or offices. Others have jobs in the government. Iranians also **manufacture** products including oil, carpets, and chemicals. Farmers grow grains, fruits, nuts, and sugar beets. They also raise livestock such as sheep.

CARPET MAKER

SHEEP HERDERS

SOCCER

WEIGHTLIFTING

Soccer has become Iran's most popular sport. Many Iranians also participate in the national sport of wrestling. Weightlifting is another well-liked activity. Skiing and snowboarding are popular activities in Iran's mountain resorts. Girls and women are getting more involved in sports, though they play separately from their male peers.

Socializing with friends and family is a popular activity in Iran. People shop in **bazaars** or meet in coffee shops and teahouses. In cities, young people go to the movies for fun. Reading is a popular pastime among Iranians. They also play games such as chess and backgammon.

CHESS

PERSIAN CARPET WEAVING

Iran is world-famous for its beautifully woven carpets. Try making your own!

What You Need:
- construction paper in various colors
- scissors
- pencil
- ruler

Instructions:
1. Take one piece of construction paper and fold it in half the long way. Draw a line parallel to the open end about 1 inch (2.5 centimeters) from the edge.

2. Use your scissors to cut from the folded end of the paper to the line. You should repeat cutting about every inch or so apart, all the way across the paper. Open the paper up so it is not folded.

3. Choose several colors of construction paper and cut 1-inch (2.5-centimeter) wide strips that are the full length of the paper. These are the weaving strips for your carpet.

4. Take one strip. Weave it under and over the layers of your paper.

5. With your next weaving strip, weave it over then under the layers of the carpet. Repeat until your carpet is full of strips!

DELICIOUS DESSERTS

Iranian cuisine includes many tasty treats. *Zoolbia* are funnel cakes soaked in a syrup made from rosewater and saffron. *Bastani* is Iranian ice cream containing rosewater, vanilla, saffron, and pistachios.

In Iran, breakfast is often simple. It might include bread, cheese, jam, walnuts, and tea. Meat, particularly lamb, is an important part of many meals. *Kebabs*, or meat grilled on sticks, are a favorite food. Rice is a **staple** in Iran. Stews are also popular. One example is *ghormeh sabzi*, which is made with lamb, herbs, and kidney beans. Iranians do not eat pork, as it is forbidden by Islam.

Iranian cooks use a variety of spices and flavorings. They include saffron, turmeric, and rosewater. Popular fruits are pomegranates, limes, and apricots. Iranians eat a lot of vegetables, and most dishes include onions.

KEBABS

GHORMEH SABZI

PERSIAN CUCUMBER YOGURT

This side dish is refreshing and easy to make. Have an adult help you prepare this delicious food.

Ingredients:
1 English cucumber
2 cups plain Greek yogurt
1/4 cup walnuts (optional)
2 tablespoons fresh mint, chopped finely
1/2 teaspoon salt
1/8 teaspoon black pepper
cucumbers, carrots, or pita bread for dipping

Steps:
1. Wash and peel the cucumber. Grate the cucumber, then use paper towels to squeeze any extra liquid out.

2. In a bowl, combine the yogurt, nuts, mint, salt, and pepper. Fold in the grated cucumber.

3. Dip vegetables or pita bread into the yogurt mixture. Enjoy!

CELEBRATIONS

Iranians celebrate many holidays. *Nouruz* marks the beginning of the Iranian New Year. It is celebrated on March 21. People visit family and exchange gifts. They also have incredible feasts. April 1 is Islamic Republic Day. This holiday marks the anniversary of when the Islamic Republic of Iran was established in 1979. People often wave flags and play **traditional** music.

Iranians celebrate many Islamic holidays. *Eid al-Fitr* is a holiday held at the end of the holy month of Ramadan. Iranians gather to pray. Then they celebrate with new clothes and festive meals. The people of Iran celebrate their country and **culture** all year long!

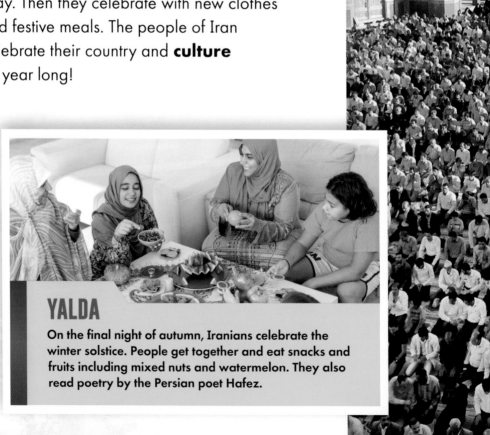

YALDA

On the final night of autumn, Iranians celebrate the winter solstice. People get together and eat snacks and fruits including mixed nuts and watermelon. They also read poetry by the Persian poet Hafez.

EID AL-FITR

642 CE
Persia becomes part
of the Islamic Empire

AROUND 4000 BCE
Iran's first great city, Susa,
becomes an urban center

1921
Reza Khan,
a Persian army officer,
seizes power

1501
Shi'a Islam becomes
the state religion

AROUND 550 BCE
Cyrus the Great begins
the first Persian Empire

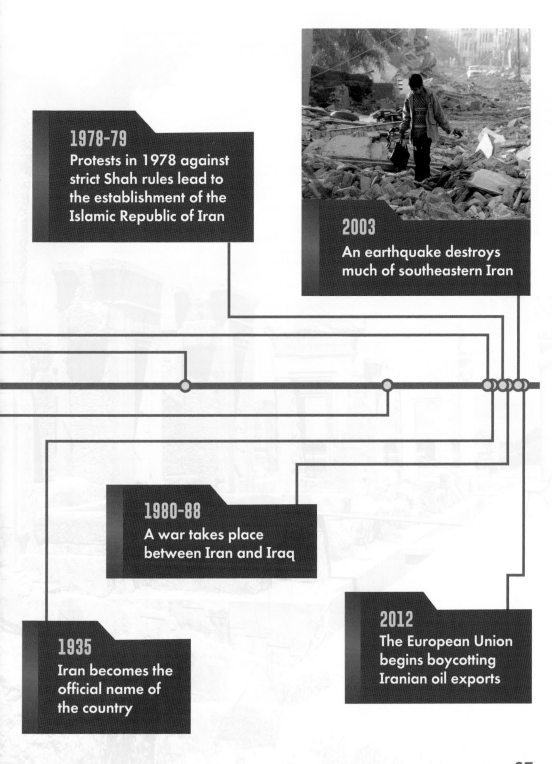

1978-79
Protests in 1978 against strict Shah rules lead to the establishment of the Islamic Republic of Iran

2003
An earthquake destroys much of southeastern Iran

1980-88
A war takes place between Iran and Iraq

1935
Iran becomes the official name of the country

2012
The European Union begins boycotting Iranian oil exports

IRAN FACTS

Official Name: Islamic Republic of Iran

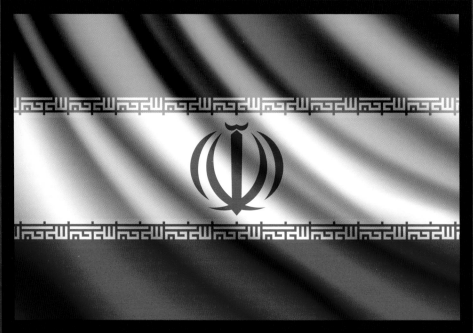

Flag of Iran: Iran's flag has three horizontal bands of color. The top band is green, the color of Islam. The middle band is white. The bottom one is red. In the center is the country's national emblem, which looks like a red tulip. Along the bottom edge of the green band and the top edge of the red band is Arabic writing which says *Allah Akbar*, meaning "God is Great."

Area: 636,372 square miles
(1,648,195 square kilometers)

Capital City: Tehran

Important Cities: Mashhad, Esfahan, Shiraz, Karaj

Population:
83,024,745 (2018)

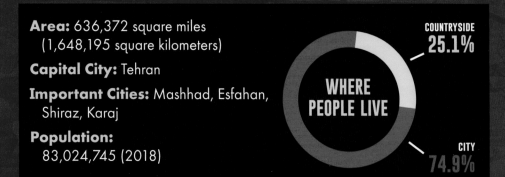

WHERE PEOPLE LIVE

COUNTRYSIDE
25.1%

CITY
74.9%

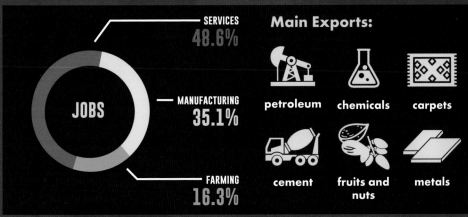

SERVICES
48.6%

JOBS

MANUFACTURING
35.1%

FARMING
16.3%

Main Exports:

petroleum

chemicals

carpets

cement

fruits and nuts

metals

National Holiday:
Republic Day (April 1)

Main Language:
Persian (official)

Form of Government:
theocratic republic

Title for Country Leaders:
supreme leader (head of state),
president (head of government)

MUSLIM
99.3%

RELIGION

OTHER
0.7%

Unit of Money:
Iranian rial

GLOSSARY

Arabs—people who are originally from the Arabian Peninsula and who now live mostly in the Middle East and northern Africa

bazaars—marketplaces containing rows of small shops or stalls

carrion—the rotting meat of dead animals

conservative—relating to traditional values and attitudes, typically in relation to religion or politics

culture—the beliefs, arts, and ways of life in a place or society

elevation—the height above sea level

ethnic—related to a group of people who share customs and an identity

manufacture—to make products, often with machines

Middle East—a region of southwestern Asia and northern Africa; this region includes Egypt, Lebanon, Iran, Iraq, Israel, Saudi Arabia, Syria, and other nearby countries.

nomadic—relating to people who have no fixed home but wander from place to place

Persian—referring to a native or resident of ancient or modern Persia, or Iran

plateau—an area of flat, raised land

rural—related to the countryside

service jobs—jobs that perform tasks for people or businesses

staple—a widely used food or other item

strait—a narrow channel connecting two bodies of water

subtropical—referring to a climate that usually has hot, humid summers and mild winters

traditional—related to customs, ideas, or beliefs handed down from one generation to the next

urban—related to cities and city life

vocational—referring to education or training directed at a particular job and its skills

TO LEARN MORE

AT THE LIBRARY

Hudak, Heather. *A Refugee's Journey from Iran.* New York, N.Y.: Crabtree Publishing Company, 2018.

Murray, Julie. *Iran.* Minneapolis, Minn.: ABDO Publishing, 2016.

Peppas, Lynn. *Cultural Traditions in Iran.* New York, N.Y.: Crabtree Publishing Company, 2015.

ON THE WEB

FACTSURFER

Factsurfer.com gives you a safe, fun way to find more information.

1. Go to www.factsurfer.com.

2. Enter "Iran" into the search box and click 🔍.

3. Select your book cover to see a list of related web sites.

INDEX

The images in this book are reproduced through the courtesy of: Nejdet Duzen, front cover; Hamdan Yoshida, pp. 4-5; Suwida Boonyatistarn, p. 5 (Badab-e Surt); arazu, p. 5 (Eram Gardens); Michal Knitl, p. 5 (Mount Damavand); Hamdan Yoshida, p. 5 (Shah Mosque); Lukas Bischoff Photograph, p. 8; Mazur Travel, p. 9 (top); Marcin Szymczak, p. 9 (bottom); Eric Isselee, p. 10 (roe deer); Erik Mandre, p. 10 (brown bear); taviphoto, p. 10 (cat snake); Alexandr Junek Imaging, p. 10 (corsac fox); Craig Lambert Photography, p. 10 (humpback whales); Viliam.M, pp. 10-11; Jon Arnold Images Ltd / Alamy Stock Photo, p. 12; Black mail Press / Alamy Stock Photo, p. 13 (top); eFesenko, p. 13 (bottom); leshiy985, p. 14; MehmetO, p. 15; ERIC LAFFORGUE / Alamy Stock Photo, p. 16, 18; Mansoreh, p. 17; Charlie Waradee, p. 19 (top); Hamed Yeganeh, p. 19 (bottom); Radiokafka, p. 20 (top); ZUMA Press / Alamy Stock Photo, p. 20 (bottom); Grigvovan , p. 21 (top); New Vibe, p. 21 (bottom); Vladimir Grigorev / Alamy Stock Photo, p. 22; hlphoto, p. 23 (top); bonchan, p. 23 (middle); Fanfo, p. 23 (bottom); Jasmin Merdan, p. 24; UPI / Alamy Stock Photo, pp. 24-25; The Print Collector / Alamy Stock Photo, p. 26 (top); North Wind Picture Archives / Alamy Stock Photo, p. 26 (bottom); Majid Saeedi / Stringer, p. 27; B.A.E Inc. / Alamy Stock Photo, p. 29 (bill); Elena Odareeva / Alamy Stock Photo, p. 29 (coin).